Sunny Rainbow Productions

NO
GREEN
EGGS
OR
HAM

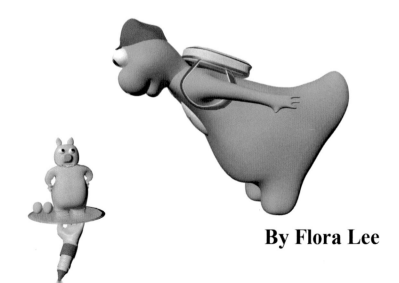

By Flora Lee

No Green Eggs Or Ham
Valen The Vegan Dinosaur Presents A parody by Flora Lee
© 2017 by Flora Lee. All rights reserved.

Published by: Sunny Rainbow Productions
Designed by: Sunny Rainbow Productions Storybook Artists

ISBN:978-1-5215728-1-8
1. Poetry 2. 3D Animation
First Edition

That Pam-I-Am.
That Pam-I-Am.
I must inform that Pam-I-Am.

Would you like green eggs or ham?

I do not eat them Pam-I-Am!
I do not eat green eggs or ham!

**Would you eat them sitting down,
On a throne, wearing a crown?**

Just look at him,
His face is frowned.

I would not eat them sitting down.
I would not eat them with a crown.
I do not like green eggs or ham.
I do not like them Pam-I-Am.

Sit down eat them with a ghost?

I would not eat them with the toast.
It's way too spooky with a ghost.

Not sitting down.
Not wearing a crown.
Not with jam.
Not with toast.
And definitely not with a ghost!

I do not want green eggs or ham!
I do not want them Pam-I-Am!

With a friend or all alone?

At the table?
On a phone?

Would you eat them knitting yarn?
Would you eat them in a barn?

Please allow me to explain,
And before you ask, not on a train.

The ham you offer, his name's Ben,
And the eggs belong to Mrs. Hen.

Now, Ben, he has a mom and dad,
And if he's gone they will feel sad.

And Mrs. Hen, those are her eggs.
They're hers to keep, just like her legs!

But, I did not want to eat alone.
I'm very hungry and on my own.

Unless...

There are more foods, just come with me,
But first let's let our friends go free.

The eggs, you say you want them green.
Chick pea flour, spinach, no need to steam.

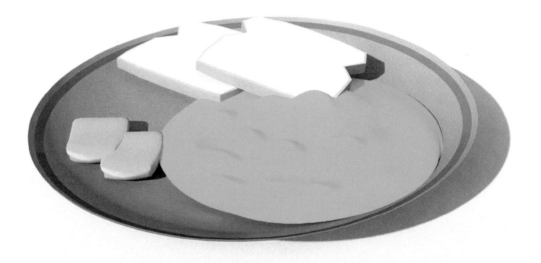

The ham, seitan is what mom would use,
Then season it with what you choose.

A taco salad, vegan cheese.
No cows were forced in making these!

A mushroom or blackbean burger.
Tasty sweet potato fries.

Mango banana ice cream.
And you'll just love the cakes and pies!

Forgive me if I'm sounding rude,
But I don't like your vegan food.

Try them!
Try them!
And you may!
Taste the food just once okay.

Valen!
I do so like what you have made!
Green eggs or ham, for this I'll trade!

Who knew dinosaurs could cook!
You must make a recipe book!

A book you say,
But, I'm just a youth.
I guess I should tell you the truth.

It's mom that bakes the cakes and muffins.
I'm not allowed to use the oven!

Be sure to check out these other great titles!

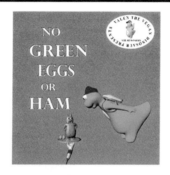

WWW.veganclubhouse.com

Made in the USA
Monee, IL
01 February 2020